SUGAR AND SPICE

A collection of poetry celebrating all things female

About the author

Carol Ellis, who writes under the pen name Mrs Yorkshire the Baking Bard, was born in 1962 in Wakefield, West Yorkshire to Irish parents.

She has been married to Michael since 1985 and they have one daughter, Jessica, born in 1991. She has been living on the Isle of Man since 2007.

She is a performing poet, infamous for her stand up style of comedy in rhyme.

Her poetry has already featured in many local and national newspapers, in magazines and on Channel 5's daytime shows *The Wright Stuff* and *The Jeremy Vine Show*.

She writes observational poetry and her cleverly-crafted poems are both humorous, witty and will have you roaring with laughter.

She also writes poetry to touch the heart and has a talent for bringing very ordinary subjects to life through the rhythmical creation of beauty in words.

Acknowledgements

To my loving husband, Michael. I can always depend on you to support me in anything I do. You give the best advice and have shown me nothing but unconditional love and encouragement.

To my darling daughter, Jessica, the inspiration for my poem *The Empty Nest*. You make me proud every day. My life improved beyond measure the day you were first placed in my arms. You proved there is no bond like the one between mother and child. Thank you for allowing me to use your superb and powerful piece of artwork to illustrate my poem 'Shame on You...' Your Grandad Ellis would be very proud of the talent you inherited from him and your dad.

To my wonderful mum, who gave me the gift of life. A lovely, nurturing mum from a long line of typical Irish mammies. You have devoted your life to your children and grandchildren and encouraged me to enjoy reading which awakened in me a love of language and writing. The poems I've written for you say it all.

To Chris Payne, who has helped, advised and guided me through the process of publishing. You have enabled me to

realise my dream. You made me believe
it could happen and made sure it did. I
am so grateful for that.

To Graeme Hogg, a wonderfully talented
and patient artist. Your illustrations
surpassed all my expectations and have
helped to bring my poetry to life. I can't
thank you enough.

And last, but by no means least, to all
my family and friends who have taken
the time to read my poetry and watched
me perform. Your unfailing support and
kind words have given me the confidence
to share my poetry.

Illustrated by Graeme Hogg

www.thewholehogg.carbonmade.com

Contents

Kids' Parties

How much do parents dread arranging their children's birthday parties? Of course, in times gone by, we were lucky to have a few mates round for tea and enjoy a couple of games of 'pin the tail on the donkey' and 'pass the parcel', followed by the obligatory ice cream and jelly. In more recent years, in the current culture of oneupmanship, parties have become more and more extravagant and ultimately more stressful for the parents. I saw a post on Facebook of a children's party and the five-year-old kids were eating sushi! I was so astounded it inspired me to write this poem.

Kids' Parties

I heard a young lady discussing, a party
for her tot
They hired a jacuzzi and served the kids
sushi
I think that they've all lost the plot!

We were happy with pass the parcel,
with only one prize for the winner
We had ice cream and jelly to fill up our
belly
And ate fish and chips for our dinner

They all want the best for their darlings,
they'll settle for nothing less
There's an awful plight over who to
invite
And it all seems a terrible stress

A professional cake is commissioned,
it's one of the main attractions
The whole decoration is quite a creation
But causes allergic reactions

Audition the entertainers, is something
they simply must do
Then the kid sees a clown and goes into
meltdown
So they opt for the petting zoo

(Cont...)

The face painter sets up his table, the
kids are most certainly eager
But three days have passed and it's still
stuck fast
And they've had to resort to Swarfega

A girl hires a nightclub or cruise ship,
the day she turns sweet sixteen
To show that they're cultured they have
an ice sculpture
And dine on the finest cuisine

Her sister's about to get married, the
nuptials are scheduled in June
I'm already dreading the forthcoming
wedding
They've hired a marquee on the moon!

The Fat Club

*So many of us try every diet going
and I'm sure there are many of you
who've joined slimming clubs, i.e.
Weight Watchers and Slimming
World. If you've never needed to go
to one of these clubs, think yourself
lucky. If you read this poem, you can
discover what goes on beyond the
dreaded weigh-in. If you've been to
one of these clubs I dare you not to
laugh out loud!*

The Fat Club

It must have been the menopause or
maybe her big bones
She was partial to Snickers, she'd
outgrown her knickers
She'd put on a couple of stones

She'd tried every fad diet going, had
even considered cocaine
But what a disaster, it made her eat
faster
Her waistband was starting to strain

So off to the fat club went Mary to
downsize her burgeoning butt
To curb her indulges and banish the
bulges
She'd turned into Jabba the Hutt

Preparing herself for the weigh-in, she
made sure she'd been to the loo
That thin, flimsy dress made her lighter
I guess
And thank goodness she'd just had a
poo

The lady in charge had a food plan, it
seemed to involve lots of greens
Making chips with *Fry Light* it was all
pretty shite
Oh she'd never get into her jeans

(Cont...)

16

Poor Susan had been to a wedding,
she'd put on two pounds in a week
She'd had a bad day but they clapped
anyway
It was rapidly looking quite bleak

To cap it all off there was Janet, she'd
managed to gain half a stone
She'd been on the booze, just come back
from a cruise
And acquired a suspected gallstone

So Janet went off to the doctors, he had
good and bad news to give
He said with a shrug, 'it's a flesh eating
bug –
But you've got 50 years left to live!'

The Mammogram

So, once we turn 50, us ladies are invited every couple of years to have a mammogram. Don't get me wrong, I strongly advise you go, but let's not kid ourselves that it's a pleasant procedure. Here's a poem I wrote about my experiences.

The Mammogram

When I was young at Catholic school I
used to say a prayer
If God would grant me my request I'd
grow a massive pair
I'd cast aside my childhood toys, my
roller skates and scooters
If I could be a lady with a decent pair of
hooters

I soon became a woman with a bit of
extra flesh
And once I'd had a baby well I could have
fed a creche
My hubby seemed to like them too and I
was chuffed to bits
Like most men he was partial to a nice
big pair of tits

I must admit I've been quite good, I've
looked after my breasts
I always took good care of them and went
for all the tests
Making sure they're in good shape, going
for a mammogram
If I was young they'd likely be a proper
hit on Instagram

(Cont...)

The letter from the clinic told me how I
must prepare
No perfume or deodorant and to tie
back all my hair
But I'm no fool, I know the score, I've
had a few before
The way to be prepared would be to slam
them in the door!

I went into a room and quickly stripped
off to the waist
And mindful of the time reported to the
nurse with haste
I ran along the corridor but little did I
know
The gown had fallen open with my
bloomin' boobs on show

Once inside I ditched the gown, got out
my double Ds
I walked up to the boob machine and
popped them on with ease
My mammaries were freezing as the
plates were cold as ice
My cups turned into saucers as it
trapped them in a vice

(Cont...)

21

I hope that in the future there's a breast
cancer vaccine
I'm sure a man invented that damn
mammogram machine
I wish I knew just who he was, I'd take
him by his nuts
And promptly place them on the plates
and squeeze them till it shuts!

The Smear Test

Now, as I'm sure I've mentioned before, it's really important that all ladies make sure they take advantage of their invitation for their regular smear test. It only takes minutes but below is a hilarious account of what it's like.

The Smear Test

I know it's not quite like me but I'm
feeling slightly stressed
Today's the day I'm due to have my
regular smear test
Flat upon my back in a position most
revealing
The nurse prepares the speculum as I
stare at the ceiling

I see that she's a proper nurse, it says so
on her badge
She's had the extra training to
investigate my vag
But still it seems a little strange, I
wonder what has made her
Decide to make a living as a qualified
womb raider

My mind begins to wander as she tells
me to relax
I think I maybe should have had that
full bikini wax
But then again, it's quite extreme, it may
be just too much
We wouldn't have to worry if they'd just
bring back the bush

(Cont...)

No sooner has she started than she's full
of doom and gloom
To complicate the matter I've a
retroverted womb
She's trying to locate it but she hasn't
found it yet
Who'd have thought my cervix would be
playing hard to get?

She's happy when she finds it, she
collects the cells and smiles
I must admit it feels as though she's
bloomin' grouting tiles
She's prodded and she's poked around in
every nook and cranny
Today has been a rotten day for me and
my poor fanny

I hurry home to make myself a nice
warm cup of tea
My hubby's there to greet me with the
kettle on for me
But then he turns to ask me as I'm filling
up the teapot
'Ay up our lass, did she locate the all
elusive G-spot?!!'

Thermostat Wars

Why do men and women disagree so much about the temperature of the house? It seems men have an in-built radiator, swanning around in their short sleeved garments, turning the heating down. Meanwhile, we're waddling around wrapped up like an eskimo. We can never seem to agree on the correct ambient temperature in the house. Here are my thoughts on the matter.

Thermostat Wars

The days are getting shorter and the
darker nights are here
The shops are getting busy too with
Christmas drawing near
Now's the time of year we're told to
spread goodwill and peace
Alas we've been invaded by the
thermostat police

Patrolling through the house just like a
bobby on the beat
Checking out the temperature and
turning down the heat
We've been turning up the dial again –
yes that's the allegation
But the only thing that's heated is the
flamin' conversation

They want to save the planet and they
say they're being green
But we don't believe a word of it, they're
only being mean
Our feet are icy cold and we are frozen
to our bones
And we'd never feel a bit of warmth if
not for our hormones

(Cont...)

We're often told to put another layer on
by our spouse
Dressed like a human duvet as we
waddle round the house
We make a pot of tea to warm our
hands up on a cuppa
And stand against the oven door while
warming up his supper

We'd wear a sexy nightie in our efforts
just to please him
Instead we're dressed in fleecy
nightwear 'cos it's flippin' freezing
We'll have to put our onesies on and
fasten them up tight
We're too cold for hanky panky and it
bloomin' serves him right!

A Birthday Poem

I'm one of life's optimists. I know this as I've been told by numerous people. I don't try to hide my age, although I have recently realised that I must stop calling myself middle-aged. After all, if I really was only half way through my life, I calculate that means I shall live until I'm 112! Here's a poem I wrote a couple of years ago on my birthday.

A Birthday Poem

Another birthday's come and gone
So long since I was twenty one
There's no point in me getting stressed
Just because I'm past my best

My hair's turned grey I cannot lie
I'm martyr to the old hair dye
I've also noticed some fine lines
And other little ageing signs

My boobs aren't bad I must agree
But they're not where they used to be
My clothes are getting awfully tight
And now I'm losing my eyesight

But I would never have believed
The lovely greetings I received
Although I'm old I just don't care
'Cos I've got friends beyond compare

Contraceptive Conundrum

I know what you're thinking, how come women have to take responsibility for contraception 99% of the time? Well if a man can't remember to put the toilet seat down after 30 years of marriage, he's not going to remember to be careful in the throes of passion. Here's a poem on the subject.

Contraceptive Conundrum

I'm sure you will agree that it's a
common misconception
That men are quite responsible when
choosing contraception
Of course the snip removes the
ammunition from the gun
To wear a vest that's bullet proof is never
any fun

Arriving at the clinic where it said 'use
the back door'
She wanted to ensure that when he
shoots he doesn't score
Early nights saved on the bills but sadly
for their sins
Instead of saving money they just ended
up with twins

She didn't like the pill, she wasn't keen
on the injection
She didn't trust the condom as a form of
contraception
The doc advised she fit the coil but what
a cheeky mare
She had a look – said she could fit a
carpet in down there

(Cont...)

She went back the next week, the doctor
fitted the Mirena*
And as she lay upon the bed she
screamed like a hyena
It felt as though the doc had shocked her
cervix with a taser
Removal five years later felt like sitting
on a razor

I'm sorry if this gloomy tale has made
you feel quite queasy
The sex life of this poor old lass was
never really easy
She once was quite a looker but the
years they took their toll
So now they leave the lights on as a form
of birth control!

(* *Mirena coil: An intra-uterine device*)

The Menopause

So, just when we think we've been through enough what with periods, pregnancy and childbirth, we hit the menopause. Let's just say it's mother nature's last joke on us poor females.

The Menopause

Well some might say the fairer sex, we
really have it tough
With periods and pregnancy you'd think
that was enough
Mother nature what a laugh – you really
are a blast
You then serve up the menopause and
save the best 'til last

Remember when our sex lives made our
toes curl, left us damp?
Well now we rarely do the deed and end
up with foot cramp
We toss and turn all night, we're all
incurable insomniacs
We used to all be nymphos but now
sadly we're just maniacs

We don't know where we parked the car
because of foggy brain
And water is the only thing these days
that we retain
Our hair is getting thinner not to
mention our dry skin
We wonder why our eyebrows have
migrated to our chin

(Cont...)

Weight gain, sagging triceps, droopy
boobs and palpitations
Frequent night trips to the loo and
other complications
Mother nature – the hot flush? That
joke is cheap and shoddy
That's not what we meant when we
requested a hot body!

So we'll grow old disgracefully and we
won't even care
Cause havoc in the nursing home, we'll
drink and smoke and swear
And when we're back in nappies and
our teeth are in a glass
We'll be shouting 'mother nature you
can kiss my wrinkly ass'!

Maggie's Hip Op

My poor old mate Maggie, who works in the local postal sorting office had to have a hip replacement. I decided to write a poem to cheer her up when she was incapacitated. Fortunately she recovered well and was soon back to her usual spritely self.

Maggie's Hip Op

A game old bird called Maggie had
some problems with mobility
Her hip it gave her gyp, it was a proper
liability
The way she limped around the town
was rather unrefined
For poor old George, her husband, it
meant no more 'bump and grind'

She worked shifts in the mail room and
you'd often hear her yelling
All those heavy sacks had caused her
stiffness and some swelling
George was still quite virile but her hip
was so worn out
That every time he mounted her she'd
do the twist and shout

She'd really had enough and it was now
becoming urgent
She booked a consultation with an
orthopaedic surgeon
Using bits of metal he said she'd be like
brand new
To her delight he told her he could
really use a screw

(Cont...)

Returning home George carried out a
sponge bath every day
It soon became quite clear that he
considered it foreplay
Tempted by the sight of her in her
compression stocking
They both succumbed and soon
enough the bed it was a-rocking

It seems they were a little over keen
with their ambitions
They went a bit too far and tried a
mixture of positions
She let him take the lead and she was
helpless in his clutches
With wild abandon she gave in and cast
aside her crutches

The neighbours weren't impressed 'cos
they were keeping them awake
Before poor Maggie fell she did the
hippy hippy shake
It really is a sorry tale the surgeon he
despaired
He's booked her in next week to have
the other hip repaired

Yummy Mummies

We've all encountered them at some point, those alpha females known as 'yummy mummies'. They turn up at the school gate and intimidate us mere mortals who still have remnants of our baby's breakfast in our hair. Here's a poem all about them.

Yummy Mummies

Dressed in trendy activewear, the posh
buggy brigade
They gave birth just two weeks ago, flat
stomachs on parade
They're training for a marathon, no
time for flabby tummies
Their prams the size of SUVs, here
come the yummy mummies

They haven't time to clean the house,
they've hired a Filipino
They meet in trendy coffee shops and
order Babyccino
Mum and baby matching togs by every
top designer
They've seen the plastic surgeon for a
lovely new vagina

Their toddlers eat organic veg and feast
on chia seeds
Employing Norland Nannies who will
see to all their needs
Weaning vegan babies can be
sometimes quite a drama
But now there's tofu baby food blessed
by the Dalai Lama

(Cont...)

They've booked a potty trainer gently
phasing out the nappy
Of course the Lego therapist makes sure
the kid is happy
Measuring their feet can sometimes see
them throwing wobblers
So they appoint a shoemaker, it's all a
load of cobblers

The moral of this story is be wary of
your staff
One such mum learned to her cost they
may have the last laugh
She wanted to impress her mates so she
employed a 'Manny'
He did a runner with her clothes, it
turned out he's a tranny

Special Delivery

*Most women go through this at least once.
They say you forget the pain, but whatever
pain you experience ever after, you always
tend to compare it to childbirth. Well if
you didn't laugh you'd cry, so I hope this
next poem makes you laugh.*

Special Delivery

She'd put a bit of timber on, she
couldn't tie her frock
She'd started feeling sick and so she
went to see the doc
Perhaps she had some kind of bug, she
had a dicky tummy
He said 'you've got Egyptian Flu –
you're going to be a mummy'

In retrospect, she told her friends, she'd
probably been reckless
She fell into his arms the night he gave
her that pearl necklace
And then she heard them say 'there
must be something in the air'
Oh yes she thought my bloomin' legs I
didn't give a care

She wouldn't be the first and it would
surely be a doddle
But morning sickness took its toll and
she began to waddle
Swollen feet, expanding boobs
conspired to make her madder
The only thing that seemed to shrink
appeared to be her bladder

(Cont...)

She visited the midwife and she peed
into a glass
And then she took her boyfriend to the
ante-natal class
The video they showed should help
prepare for the bambino
Alas it was just like a film by Quentin
Tarantino

They had to break her waters and it
wasn't looking good
Niagara Falls fell from her flue in one
almighty flood
By now she'd had enough of doctors
sticking gadgets up it
She'd had so many hands up her she felt
like a glove puppet

It seemed her reproductive parts had
come under attack
She felt as though Bruce Lee had
bloomin' kicked her in the back
The midwife got the scissors out then
in came 'Doc the Ripper'
With one terrific scream at last she
gave birth to the nipper

(Cont...)

The damage was quite bad and so she'd
have to be re-built
She feared her lady garden would be like
a patchwork quilt
The midwife started sewing and it went
without a hitch
Until her boyfriend said that she could
use an extra stitch!

Retro Fitness

In the struggle to keep fit in middle age I joined a dance class. Well, I'm not really into all that weight lifting and I thought I might as well do something I enjoy. Once a week I get to pretend I'm 18 again and in a nightclub in Wakefield dancing around my handbag to the music of the day. Here's a humorous poem about my endeavours to maintain and recapture my youth.

Retro Fitness

Reflecting on when she was only a teen
She would boogie all night like a true
'Dancing Queen'
She could turn a few heads in that short
ra-ra skirt
'Cos her thighs were quite firm and her
boobs were still pert

Meeting her mates all dressed up in
their glad rags
Down at the nightclub they'd dance
round their handbags
It's sad that she can't strut her stuff like
before
She's to think of the strain on her old
pelvic floor

She considered the gym but she'd then
need to wax
To compete with the babes and their
matching six packs
She saw the equipment and wasn't too
keen
She was only impressed by the chocolate
machine

(Cont...)

Removing her apron she set aside
baking
She pulled on her leggings to go booty
shaking
A dance class was better than just
staying in
These days she went out even less than
her bin

The lady in charge was so young and
attractive
Between you and me she seemed quite
hyperactive
She played disco music from halcyon
days
When shoulder pads, boob tubes and
perms were the craze

In no time at all they were soon 'body
popping'
And to her surprise they were even 'slut
dropping'
The shapes they were throwing would
make a nun blush
An old lass at the back had a sudden hot
flush

It's quickly become the best night of her
week
Even though some say she's now passed
her peak
She's jumping around like a frisky young
pup
At least when she gets down she can
now get back up!

Haute Cuisine

Have you noticed the current trend for this 'haute cuisine'? In other words half as much food for twice the price. Chips served in a cup instead of being piled high on your plate? Here's a poem about a meal out with my husband. It's written from his point of view so, altogether now, in your best Yorkshire accents...

Haute Cuisine

I'm married to a Yorkshire girl, she's not
a bad old lass
She's always tea ont table and she's careful
wi' mi brass
She dunt spend owt on alcohol, she'd
rather 'ave a bun
And being vegetarian, she's proper cheap
to run

To celebrate her birthday, I took her for
a treat
And as it's only once a year, I thought I'd
do it reet
I dusted off mi wallet and I took her into
pub
And feeling proper generous, I bought
our lass some grub

She's allus on a diet so she's never eaten
much
Although I like a well-stacked lass who's
softer to the touch
I told her 'get thi snout in trough', dint
want her getting thinner
And I was feeling famished and was
ready for mi dinner

(Cont...)

But when the grub arrived well now the
portions were quite mean
The waitress duly told me this was
known as 'haute cuisine'
'Eee by gum tha must be daft' I said in
my defence
'Tha must think that I'm sackless and I've
got more brass than sense'

The chips were in a teacup you could
count 'em on one hand
And why the veg was rationed I just
couldn't understand
By 'eck it soon transpired that they were
then expecting tips
I gave 'em one – I told 'em to stop
skimping on the chips

So on our anniversary I 'ave a cunning
plan
I'll tek her on a day trip 'cos I'm such a
thoughtful man
Before we start ont journey, like a wise
and prudent chap
I'll set her on int kitchen and we'll tek us
bloomin' snap!

A Woman's World

I was privileged enough to appear on Channel 5's The Wright Stuff on International Women's Day 2018, reading this poem out via video link. Instead of worrying about what people think of us, or how we should be conforming to a distorted media perception of physical beauty, we should embrace our bodies, hearts and minds. After all, they do some pretty awesome things. Let's hear it for the girls!

A Woman's World

Don't tell me I'm imperfect I am perfect
as I am
Your judgement counts for nothing as I
just don't give a damn
A female with a point of view will always
be in fashion
The beauty of a woman's in her heart,
her soul, her passion

My body is unique, I love the rolls, the
curves, the dips
The wobble of my ageing flesh, the
roundness of my hips
Creating and sustaining life, is worthy of
great awe
And why have just one orgasm, I'm
capable of more!

A woman with a purpose is much
stronger than she thinks
She looks a challenge in the eye and
confidently winks
There's nothing that can stop her if she's
truly on a mission
Her fundamental attribute is female
intuition

(Cont...)

My roles are often varied, I've been
known to multi-task
A wife, a mum, a daughter I just wear a
different mask
A woman was created to be loved, not
understood
We really rock the world, let's celebrate
our womanhood!

Shame on You...

This is a very special poem that I've only just written. I posted this on my Facebook page and it's by far the most liked, shared and commented on poem I've ever posted. It has gone viral around the world, such is the strength of feeling about the subject matter. A criminal trial in Ireland, in which the lawyer of a man accused of rape cited the lacy underwear worn by a woman as a sign of her consent, has ignited outrage across the country and beyond. A lacy thong doesn't cause rape – rapists cause rape. Thank you to my very talented daughter, Jessica, for allowing me to use her extremely powerful piece of artwork.

Shame on You...

Battered, broken, raped, abused
Injured party stands accused
Vicious culture of slut shame
Acceptable to victim blame

She'd had a drink, her skirt was short
She liked to flirt, was just the sort
'She asked for it' you'll hear them say
'Boys will be boys' so that's OK

But that's not how the story went
He never cared about consent
And now it seems she'll serve her time
Trapped inside the scene of the crime

A wedding ring, a sexy dress
A lacy thong does not mean yes
Impossible to misconstrue
That 'no means no' so shame on you...

The Rhyme of My Life: The story of Mrs Yorkshire the Baking Bard

Night Mail poem

So when did all this 'poetry malarkey' begin? Well, when I was in the second year of high school we read a poem by W H Auden, *Night Mail*. You may be familiar with the poem.

At the time there were problems with the roof of our high school so the first and second year pupils were re-located to a disused Victorian school near the city centre. The classrooms had large windows which were located above head height, preventing children

Ings Road School, Wakefield

from daydreaming out of the window or being distracted by the world outside. It was a late afternoon lesson and by now my thoughts were turning to catching the bus home with friends. Beams of sun boldly streamed into the room and I watched the dust particles dancing within them, willing the time to pass.

Our English teacher began reading the poem and suddenly I was transfixed. The rhythm of the poem conjured up the image of the train bustling through the British night-time countryside. I wanted to be able to write poetry like that. I'd read books and pieces of prose but this was something else. This was like dancing instead of walking.

The ability to connect with someone, anyone, whether friends or strangers, through the power of words, both fascinated and thrilled me in equal measure.

In that moment I realised that through the use of language in all its beauty and different forms, I could reach into the hearts and minds of people and make them laugh, cry, contemplate, examine, reflect and ultimately share my passion for the words and their message.

Our homework was set – to write a poem in the same style. A train journey, any train journey of our choice. I could see my classmates were packing their books away. To them it was just the end of another boring lesson. I felt detached from my surroundings. My mind was racing. I was already thinking about what I was going to write.

I queued up for the school bus. I was the chatterbox of the group and often led the conversation which usually revolved around pop music, fashion, a TV programme or techniques implemented to achieve the latest hairstyle, but I was still distracted. Words and rhymes were already running around my head in anticipation of writing my poem.

I ran into the house and as usual we gathered round the table for our tea. It was a busy, noisy house. Four children and two adults. There was always plenty of activity. People coming and going. The constant clatter of pots and pans from the kitchen. Radio Eireann blasting out Irish music, my mum singing along and my father occasionally playing his tin whistle. There were the usual altercations, raised voices and doors slamming.

I shared a bedroom with my older sister but fortunately this evening she was otherwise engaged watching TV downstairs, which was just as well because there was an unwritten rule that being the oldest she was in charge. It was primarily her bedroom. Most evenings the whole family would huddle round the fire in the living room to watch TV as there was no central heating in the house. Some evenings I braved the cold in my bedroom to listen to Radio Luxembourg on a transistor radio, a pop music station which broadcasted on 208 medium wave every evening during the 1970s. The DJ, Tony Prince, or my favourite, 'Kid' Jensen, would host *The Battle of the Bands* – the *Bay City Rollers vs The Osmonds* or *David Cassidy vs David Essex*. My sister sometimes listened with me.

If I had enough pocket money I'd buy the *Fabulous 208* magazine which listed the song lyrics of all my favourite artists of the day. I'd carefully remove the staples from the centre pages and place the full colour poster spread across the middle pages on the wall above my bed.

I relished the fact that I had the bedroom to myself and wasted no time in retrieving my English homework book from my school bag which I'd thrown hastily on the bed. I had to kneel on the floor against the bed, my legs tucked underneath me, using the bed as a makeshift desk. The candlewick bedspread against my body and legs kept me warm and I'd closed the door to block out the noise from the rest of the family downstairs. I remembered the poem by Auden. As the teacher read it aloud I'd heard the underlying rhythm, mimicking the sound of a train on the tracks.

I began writing and found the ability to use the correct amount of stressed and unstressed syllables in each line came easily to me, as though I was singing a song. Once I started writing it was a like a tap had been turned on in my head. The words came flowing out, spilling onto the page. An exhilarating journey of creativity and self-discovery.

I was pleased with my efforts and duly handed my homework in. A couple of days later at the beginning of the lesson the English teacher moved around the room, skilfully dodging the school bags carelessly discarded on the floor, as if negotiating an army assault course. He shouted out each pupil's mark as he handed back their homework. Sometimes he paused and made comments: 'good effort', 'watch your spelling'. I waited impatiently for my homework to be returned until he only had one book left in his hand.

As he returned to his desk a wave of panic rose within me. Had I misunderstood the instructions and written something completely different to everyone else? A sudden rush of heat enveloped me and I sat up straight in my chair, arms folded in front of me as if to protect myself from the inevitable onslaught of humiliation and mortification.

After what seemed like an age he held my book up and proceeded to inform the class that he wanted to read my poem to everyone as an example of the correct interpretation of the homework set! He was very impressed by my use of metre and rhyme. He told the class to listen to the rhythm as he read.

My face still burned like a hot pan on a stove, the anticipation of hearing my poem read aloud bubbling inside me. An extraordinary sense of elation swept over me as I listened to him read the poem, just as I'd intended it to be read. I could hear the rhythm of the train – my train, not the train with the *Night Mail,* but the one I'd envisaged rattling along the tracks through verdant countryside on a warm summer's day.

I felt dizzy with delight. I wanted to close my eyes and savour the moment. All eyes were upon me. There were audible gasps and murmurs of appreciation.The ball in my throat threatened to escape my lips. I burned with a fierce joy.

That was just the beginning of my love affair with language and words. Whenever the teacher asked us to write a story for homework, I became completely engrossed. Nothing else was important. During the subsequent lessons I became distracted. My mind was like a butterfly fluttering back to the story I'd already started writing in my head.

By the time I reached the fourth year I had a different but no less encouraging English teacher. His name was Mr Devlin. He always read my stories to the class. I think he appreciated my enthusiasm, even though I was a 'lively' member of the class, partial to a fair amount of giggling and chattering.

Age 16, centre of photo

71

One day, as we were filing past his desk to go to the next lesson, he stopped me and told me I had a gift and I musn't waste it. A gift? What did that mean to a 15-year-

St Thomas à Becket School

old girl, and what did he mean that I musn't waste it? OK so I could write a good story, tell a good tale, but I put that down to my Irish upbringing. I was from a working class family and shouldn't get ideas above my station. I'd leave school, maybe go to college, get a job, meet a nice young man, get married and start a family.

And that's exactly what I did. I left school, went to secretarial college, got a job, met a nice young man, got married and had a daughter. I still read books when I had the time. Occasionally, if someone was leaving work or having a special birthday, I wrote a poem. I didn't even bother to keep copies.

Once I became a mother it was all-consuming. I wanted to recreate *The Little House on the Prairie*. To be the perfect wife and mother. To indulge my child with my time and make her childhood as magical as possible. To be an accomplished housekeeper and cook. 'She always keeps a good table'. That's what I used to hear when I was growing up.

Eventually my husband, Michael and I,

together with our daughter, Jessica, re-located from Yorkshire to live on the Isle of Man.

Maughold Village, Isle of Man

A couple of years later Jessica went across the sea to Queen's University in Belfast and suddenly there was just the two of us. I was in my late forties. She left university, got a job and settled in the north of Ireland. We had an empty nest and our thoughts turned to slowing down and not working so many hours.

We were running our small mail order company together when my husband returned to working in advertising. We scaled the mail order company down and essentially I was working part time.

At the top of Maughold Head

I missed my daughter terribly and felt it would be a good distraction to indulge myself a little. I started walking for pleasure and fitness. I baked cakes for friends and family. Whatever the occasion I'd turn up with a cake!

I was sitting down one day, my thoughts turning to life on the Isle of Man and all its quirks and curiosities. We would have been living here nine years in just over a month. I started to write, not with

Selling my cupcakes

a pen but with a keyboard. My fingers danced skilfully across the keys as ideas popped into my head. It was like an epiphany, I could write a poem to celebrate because I could write poetry! Of course I could write poetry, I used to write poetry, why hadn't I written poetry for so long?

I read the poem to my husband. He thought it was very good. Would he have dared tell me if it was rubbish? I wasn't too sure. My friend Sonia came round. She's a straight talking Geordie lass. Kind but honest. She listened intently and when I'd finished she said it was brilliant. She encouraged me to post it on Facebook.

I still wasn't convinced and read it to a couple of other people who were similarly impressed. Sonia beseeched me to post the poem on Facebook so that others could enjoy and appreciate it, particularly our friends on the island. After much deliberation, a month later, on the ninth anniversary of moving here, I took the plunge and posted the poem on my Facebook page.

I was like that 13-year-old girl again, filled with uncertainty and anticipation. However, within minutes the poem was being commented on favourably and shared all over Facebook. Of course, I still doubted myself: after all, these were my friends. They wouldn't be cruel enough to criticise the composition I'd carefully created and crafted for their enjoyment. I wrote a couple more poems and these too were received very positively.

A few months later I joined the Isle of Man Poetry Society. I hadn't even realised there was one except a friend told me about it. I went along to the meeting with only three poems in my folder.

A group of people were sitting around a large table. Each member read a poem to the group, either one that they'd written or one from a book. I began to think I'd probably made a mistake as the poetry didn't appear to be in the same vein as mine. Oh dear, what would they make of my poetry? There was to be a break for coffee half-way through and I considered leaving quietly through the back door.

Just before we broke for coffee a gentleman began reading one of his own compositions. As he began reading I felt relief wash over me. His poetry was a very similar style to mine.

The chairperson asked if I had anything I'd like to read so I nervously retrieved my poem about the Isle of Man from my folder and began to read. It's a humorous and affectionate poem entitled *The Come Over.*

They appeared to be laughing in all the correct places. I finished and held my breath. Everyone clapped. Thank goodness – I hadn't offended anyone and they actually appeared to enjoy my poetry.

We had coffee and I chatted to the gentleman who read before me. He was there with his wife, also a talented poet.

It transpired that he was something of a local celebrity. He wrote a column in the Manx Independent, the island's main newspaper, and featured on local radio once a week. Indeed, much like Cher, Cilla and Lulu, he was known by only one name: 'Pullyman'. I felt I was in the presence of some rather special people.

In the second half of the meeting another gentleman began reading his own poetry. This blew my mind. He appeared to have an encyclopaedic knowledge of rhyming and metre schemes and this was reflected in his poetry which was both witty and superbly written.

After the meeting the gentleman, whose name is Dennis Turner, approached me and asked if he could discuss my poetry with me as he enjoyed it very much. His words were 'I think you've got something'.

I met with Dennis and we chatted over my homemade cake and a cup of Yorkshire Tea. He spoke to me about my use of 'feminine endings'. I didn't even know there was such a thing but apparently I was using these to great effect!

I felt honoured that he was imparting his knowledge to me. He said he couldn't really teach me anything as I instinctively followed the rules of good metre and rhyme but he wanted me to know why I was doing what I did.

I was like a child, hungry for knowledge and eager to learn. He began talking about iambic, trochaic, spondaic and dactylic metres. He explained the use of stressed and unstressed syllables. I vaguely remembered some of it from school. Poetry became increasingly fascinating.

I know his in-depth knowledge of metre and rhyme which he has so generously shared with me and continues to do so, inspires me to this day and has improved my writing beyond measure.

Through the Poetry Society meetings I discovered the poetry Open Mic events which take place on the island. These are organised by another very talented poet called Hazel Teare. Hazel also comperes these evenings.

Performing with IOM poets

I'd enjoyed amateur dramatics at school and quite often took the lead role in school productions. Maybe this was because I had a loud voice, but either way I figured this would come in handy at the Open Mic events and for performing in public!

Performing as a witch, age 15

The Open Mic events have grown in such popularity that spectators are regularly turned away as they're full to capacity. They've also given me the opportunity to hone my performance skills considerably.

Performing at Manx Litfest

Hazel started the Open Mic evenings a few years before to give anyone wishing to perform their poetry a platform. It was a kind of rebellion against the stuffy academic image poetry has and the idea that only academics can successfully produce good poetry. Making poetry accessible to all is the key to their success.

Performing at the Isle of Man Hospice 35th Anniversary event for volunteers, Douglas

Once I became involved with the poetry scene on the island I soon began performing at local charity events and private functions. I tailor my poetry to suit the audience and find the more I perform the easier it becomes.

I decided to create a public Facebook page to share my poetry and that's when I came up with the idea for a pen name. Since living on the island I've become known as *Mrs Yorkshire* as I'm instantly recognisable by my accent. I'm also well-known for my baking skills so I put the two together and came up with *Mrs Yorkshire the Baking Bard.*

The page enabled me to connect with poetry lovers from all over the world. As I write observational poetry on all subjects, I've been able to share poems of specific interest to certain groups and attract more followers.

On special occasions I share relevant poetry. At Christmas I share my poem *Carol for Christmas*. On Valentine's Day I share my poem *A Yorkshire Valentine* and, of course, I always share my *Halloween* poem on 31st October. During the year there are many other special days such as St Patrick's Day, Yorkshire Day, Breast Cancer Awareness month – the list is endless.

Facebook: Mrs Yorkshire the Baking Bard

I also began writing poetry with certain days in mind. On National Poetry Day a couple of years ago I wrote a poem and posted it to Channel 5's daytime TV show *The Wright Stuff*. I was stunned when they actually read it out live on air.

I wrote a poem to celebrate International Women's Day and this time Matthew Wright, the presenter of the show, contacted me and asked me if I'd like to video the poem so that I could read it myself on the show! I was absolutely delighted and duly did so.

The Wright Stuff

A few months later it was announced he was leaving the show after eighteen years.

I was so grateful for his kindness that I sent him good wishes and wrote a few lines in verse to wish him well.

The Wright Stuff

Matthew contacted me again and asked if I'd be kind enough to video the poem to feature on his final show. I was honoured and delighted to do this. I've since appeared on *The Jeremy Vine Show*, which replaced *The Wright Stuff*, reading a poem for National Poetry Day again.

I've also had my poems published in many local and national newspapers and magazines.

My husband, Michael, convinced me that I should set up a Youtube channel so I've made videos of a few of my poems and uploaded them onto there too. Go to youtube.com and type in 'Mrs Yorkshire' to view the videos on my channel.

During this time a very good friend of ours came to visit us on the island. Chris Payne is a very successful and highly respected businessman who began his career in marketing in the 1980s. He has worked as a reviews editor, mainly for computer magazines, and created Europe's largest mail order supplier of light and sound machines including lucid dreaming machines and other devices. He's currently the Managing Director of Effort-Free

Media Ltd, helping consultants, trainers and coaches to create quality e-products they can give away and sell.

Chris had been reading my poetry online and watching my videos on my Youtube channel. He encouraged me to publish my poetry. I told him it was a dream of mine to publish a book and he convinced me that, with his help, it would happen. He advised me to write a trilogy of books, each of the three books on a different theme, and suggested that each poem should have an illustration to accompany it.

I was lucky enough to find a very talented, experienced and highly respected artist and illustrator, Graeme Hogg at *The Whole Hogg*. His illustrations have brought my poetry to life. I never even considered illustrating the books but I'm so pleased I did. You can have a look at more of Graeme's work on his web site https://thewholehogg.carbonmade.com/. You won't be disappointed.

So, after not even three years of re-discovering my love of poetry, here I am publishing a trilogy of poetry books. I'm 56 years old and have realised it's never too late to follow your dreams and make them come true. I've had a lot of support and encouragement and made lots of friends along the way.

My books are available to purchase

separately or as a trilogy at a reduced price. If you've purchased any of my books from Amazon, please leave me feedback in the reviews. It's great to connect with my readers.

I'm always open to requests to write on any subject, so if you think there's something I should write about, drop me a line and tell me!

You can write to me at c/o Red Lizard Ltd, PO Box 18, Ramsey, Isle of Man, British Isles, IM99 4PG, e-mail me at carolellis2012@gmail.com, or message me through my Facebook page: *Mrs Yorkshire the Baking Bard.*

I'm happy to post signed copies of books. I accept commissions to write poetry to order. If you have a specific event or celebration, as long as I have a few details regarding the person you'd like the poem for, I can come up with something especially for them. I'm also happy to perform at corporate and charity events, social functions and engage in TV and radio appearances.

I have a book stuffed full of ideas for poems, all waiting to be written. If there were more hours in the day I could fill them writing poetry. I know I'll never run out of things to write about if I live to be over 100 years old!

Thank you for reading my poetry. My original dream as a 13-year-old girl was to share my love of words with the world and, finally, I believe that dream has come true.

Carol Ellis
Mrs Yorkshire the
Baking Bard
X

Useful information

Although the poems in this book
are mostly humorous, the subjects
covered affect many women.

Although I've made light of
mammograms and smear tests,
it is very important that women
take advantage of any preventative
treatments available.

There's also support for many
other issues such as childbirth,
contraception, sexual health,
parenting and, of course, the
menopause.

Overleaf is a list of useful contacts.

www.breastcancercare.org.uk
0808 800 6000

www.macmillan.org.uk/information-
and-support/cervical-cancer

www.letstalkaboutit.nhs.uk/
contraception/

www.nhs.uk/using-the-nhs/nhs-
services/sexual-health-services/guide-
to-sexual-health-services/

www.nct.org.uk

www.menopausesupport.co.uk/

88

www.rapecrisis.org.uk

www.rcni.ie

Web sites, helplines and support groups for parents:

Contact a Family

Support, advice and information for parents with disabled children.
Helpline: 0808 808 3555
Web site: www.cafamily.org.uk

Family Lives

An organisation providing immediate help from volunteer parent support workers, 24 hours a day, 7 days a week
Helpline: 0808 800 2222
Web site: www.familylives.org.uk

Family Rights Group

Support for parents and other family members whose children are involved with or in need of social care services
Helpline: 0808 801 0366
Web site: www.frg.org.uk

Gingerbread: single parents, equal families

Help and advice on the issues that matter to lone parents.
Helpline: 0808 802 0925
Web site: www.gingerbread.org.uk

(Cont...)

Parent and Baby Groups

To find out about local groups:

Ask your health visitor or GP.

Look on noticeboards and for leaflets at your local child health clinic, health centre, GP's waiting room, children's centre, library, advice centre, supermarket, newsagent or toy shop. Look for local Facebook support groups.

In some areas there are groups that offer support for parents of the same background and culture. Many of these are women's or mothers' groups.

Lots of children's centres also run fathers' groups and groups for teenage parents. Your health visitor may know if there are any groups like these near you.

Also available

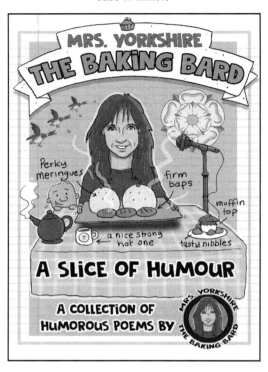

Mrs Yorkshire the Baking Bard
c/o Red Lizard Ltd
PO Box 18
Ramsey
Isle of Man
IM99 4PG

carolellis2012@gmail.com

Facebook: Mrs Yorkshire the Baking Bard

YouTube: Mrs Yorkshire

Give it a Go

Why not have a go at writing your own poetry? I believe you can write a poem about any subject. Write down a few ideas about what you'd like to say about your subject matter and let each idea form a verse.

If you're stuck for a rhyme, use the 'Rhymezone' web site, it's far more useful than going through the alphabet in your head, chanting rhyming words!

As you've probably gathered, I like to write rhyming poetry with good, structured metre. Metre is the basic rhythmic structure of a verse or lines in a poem. I find poetry with structured metre much easier to recite and much easier for the reader to read too. If you're in doubt about whether a line 'scans', even after you've read it back, count the number of syllables in each line to see if they match. You may need to swap one word for another so that it fits. A Thesaurus is very useful for this. There is a web site called *Thesaurus* to make it easier for you.

I've left a few blank pages at the back of this book for you to write down your ideas and, who knows, you may release

your inner poet. Go on, give it a go.
You may find you enjoy writing poetry
as much as reading it.

Why not write a poem about
something we can all relate to? You
can make it humorous, sentimental,
thought-provoking – the possibilities
are endless. Overleaf I've written the
first couple of lines of the poem to
start you off. Keep your verses to four
lines each in rhyming couplets. Good
luck!

Mrs Yorkshire the Baking Bard x

Here are the first two lines of a poem to inspire you to write the rest. Good luck!

Women's Intuition

Did you ever wonder why a woman's
always right?
She appears to be have the power to
possess a second sight

Printed in Poland
by Amazon Fulfillment
Poland Sp. z o.o., Wrocław